This book belongs to:

Look Before You Bounce

Disney's Out & About With Pooh

A Grow and Learn Library

Published by Advance Publishers
© 1996 Disney Enterprises, Inc.
Based on the Pooh stories by A. A. Milne © The Pooh Properties Trust.

Written by Ronald Kidd
Illustrated by Arkadia Illustration Ltd.
Designed by Vickey Bolling
Produced by Bumpy Slide Books

ISBN:1-885222-58-0
10 9 8 7 6 5 4 3 2 1

One morning when Tigger woke up, his eyebrows were twitching. The twitch traveled along his nose to his mouth, where it became a grin. From there it spread down his neck and around his stripes.

By the time it reached his tail, it had turned into a bounce.

Tigger flew into the air, his arms spread wide.
"I'm bouncin'!" he cried. "Look at me bounce!"
He bounced higher and higher, until the place where he was bouncing seemed a bit too small. So he bounced down the path and into the forest.

Not far away, Rabbit was picking carrots. Being a neat, tidy Rabbit, he sorted the carrots as he picked them. He put the big carrots in one pile and the little carrots in another pile.

Sometimes a carrot wasn't big enough or little enough to belong in either pile. When this happened, Rabbit acted quickly and ate the carrot in a few bites.

Rabbit was happily munching on a carrot, admiring his work, when he saw something out of the corner of his eye. It was big and orange. For one delicious moment Rabbit thought it might be a giant carrot.

Then he looked more closely and saw that the big orange thing had stripes and a grin. It was Tigger, and he was headed straight for Rabbit's neat carrot piles.

"Watch out!" cried Rabbit, but it was too late. Tigger knocked over the piles, mixing the big carrots with the little carrots and scattering them everywhere.

Rabbit moaned, "Tigger, what are you doing?"

"Bouncin'!" said Tigger. "Want to see me do it again?"

"No, I do not!" said Rabbit. Then he explained that while bouncing might be fun, it could also cause problems for others if you didn't watch where you were going.

"Carrots aren't the only thing you could land on," Rabbit said. "The forest is filled with plants and animals, so you have to be careful."

"Why, being careful is what tiggers do best!" Tigger said as he bounced off through the trees. Rabbit chased after him, calling, "Now, remember — look before you bounce!"

In another part of the forest, Pooh was feeling proud of himself. He had always thought he was the slowest animal in the forest, but today he had found an animal that was even slower. It was a turtle.

As Pooh watched the turtle inch its way up the path, he felt positively speedy. To celebrate, he sang a speedy sort of song.

I won't finish last
Because I'm so fast.
Why, even my song
Doesn't take long!

As Pooh finished his song, someone came bouncing along who was even faster than he was. It was Tigger, and he didn't seem to notice the turtle in his path. Pooh waved for him to stop, but Tigger still wasn't paying attention. Tigger bounced into the turtle, and the two of them went sprawling across the ground.

Speedy bear that he was, Pooh leapt into action and checked to see if the turtle was all right. "Oh, no!" cried Pooh with alarm. "Its head and legs are missing!"

Rabbit hurried over. "Don't worry," he told his friends. "When danger nears, turtles pull their heads and legs inside their hard, sturdy shells. That's how they keep the soft parts of their bodies safe."

As Pooh watched, the turtle stuck out its head to see if the coast was clear. A moment later, it went lumbering off down the path.

Rabbit turned to Tigger. "Please, please, Tigger! Watch where you're going next time."

"Of course!" Tigger replied. "Watching is what tiggers do best!" Then he hopped to his feet and bounced off once again.

Farther down the path, Piglet was making a new friend. It was black and furry, with a white stripe down its back. Piglet noticed that the animal seemed nervous and was stamping its feet. Not wanting to upset the creature, Piglet spoke in a quiet, gentle voice.

Suddenly Tigger came crashing through the bushes, with Rabbit and Pooh following close behind. When Rabbit saw Piglet's friend, a strange look crossed his face.

"Run!" he cried to the others. "Run as fast as you can!"

Tigger, Pooh, Piglet, and Rabbit headed for the trees.
As they did, the frightened animal sprayed a cloud of
terrible-smelling mist.

When they were a safe distance away, Rabbit explained, "Piglet's new friend is a skunk, and that awful spray is his way of chasing off anyone he thinks might hurt him."

"He doesn't need to worry!" Tigger said confidently.
"Staying away is what tiggers do best!" And off he bounced.

In a gloomy part of the forest, Eeyore was eating thistles. There were prickles and needles on the leaves, but Eeyore didn't mind.

The donkey moved through the thistle patch, munching as he went, when all of a sudden there was a BOING! BOING! BOING!

He looked up and saw Tigger, trailed by Rabbit, Pooh, and Piglet.

"Yippee," said Eeyore in his slow, mournful voice. "I love a parade."

The odd thing about this parade was that it was headed straight for Eeyore. In fact, it looked as if it would run right into him.

"Oh, well," said Eeyore.

Then something surprising happened. The front of the parade, which was Tigger, didn't run into him after all. It bounced in the thistle patch and went rocketing toward the sky, crying, "Yeeowww!"

"Oh, bother," said Pooh, looking around. "I think we've lost Tigger."

But Tigger wasn't lost at all. He was high in the air, on the biggest bounce of his life. When he came down, he did lots of little bounces all around his friends.

"Hello, Tigger," said Pooh, smiling. "We're glad to have you back."

But Tigger didn't seem very happy at all.

Piglet asked, "Why is Tigger holding his paw?"
"Because he bounced on a thistle," Rabbit replied.
When Tigger finally stopped bouncing, they gathered
around to look at his paw. Sure enough, they found a prickle
from a thistle leaf. Rabbit gently removed it, and Pooh
rubbed a little honey on the spot to make it feel better.

Rabbit said, "I'm sorry, Tigger, but I tried to warn you. You need to be careful when you go bouncing through the forest."
"If you bother a turtle, it will hide inside its shell," said Pooh.

"If you frighten a skunk, it might spray you," said Piglet.

"And if you land on a thistle, you could hurt your paw," said Eeyore. "Besides that, you could ruin my dinner."

"Animals have ways of protecting themselves," Rabbit explained, "and so do plants. Thistles protect themselves with prickles. Rose bushes have thorns. Cactus plants have spikes. It's just their way of saying—"

"I know," said Tigger. "Look before you bounce!"

Grinning at his friends, Tigger said, "Thanks for taking care of my paw. I'd stay longer, but I've got more bouncin' to do. Ta-ta for now!"

Once again, Tigger was off to the forest. But this time, on the advice of his friends, he was careful to do one very important thing.

He looked before he bounced.